Lifeskills

for

Teens

A COMPREHENSIVE GUIDE TO MANAGING YOUR FINANCES: MONEY, BUDGETING, COOKING, SOFT SKILLS, AND MENTAL KNOWLEDGE

By

Annie James

Table of Contents

1

Valuable Skills

Life skills are super important and useful in everyday life. With It, you feel you have superpowers to do every work quickly, and they can be learned.

A good education teaches basic skills needed in life. Teens should grow beyond the college degree. This is important as we make relationships, personalities and careers in our lives.

We learn valuable skills in schools but there are more.

Skills like critical thinking, managing money, budgeting, solving real-world problems and so on. When you get them, you will be ready for the challenges ahead.

Parents, teachers or society should get ready.

 "It takes a village to raise a child" is gotten from an African proverb and it means that many are involved in providing a secure, healthy and growth filled atmosphere for kids and teens. This is how you will realize your dreams and aspiration.

Examples of valuable skills that we can learn at home or school.

- **Cooking Your Meals**– you can make this anytime you want.

- <u>**Making New Friends**</u> – making good friends is a vital skill you need to master. You will have more friends to play with and fun you can be with at any time.

- **Solving Mathematical problems** – you will learn how to perform simple problem-solving skills when you're stuck

- **Handling Emotional Stress** so you stay calm when things get out of control.
  Life skills also help you outside of school, like at home or church or an event. You will learn lots of adulting things.

These skills are better learned at an early age.
Now, you can start building your life skills.

These life skills need to be covered in school. So, how do you gain this practical knowledge?

This book is an excellent place to start, and you should follow it up by getting involved in practical exercises outlined at the end of each chapter.

The knowledge taught in traditional schooling has little applicability in the real world. But there is always time to take control of your learning and build practical life skills.

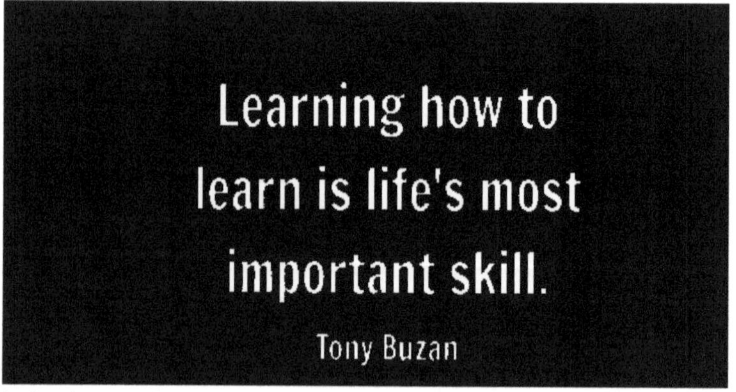

The right knowledge is a good step in the right direction. You can learn to make good choices, resolve quarrels, and believe in yourself. That's the education we need.

2

Healthy Eating Skills

Teens have to make so many food choices each day, knowing what food category and list is good for you require some set of skills. It's hard to resist cravings for delicious snacks and unhealthy ones. That's the reason

why in this chapter, we shall cover the reasons for such occurrence and how to eat healthy, and strong.

School curriculum and extra classes may lead to teens skipping their meals or prepare a quick fix during breakfast and dinner. I understand. Most teens need fast foods and will want to avoid any stress related to making a proper diet. This attitude will affect their growth as the body will try to make up for any nutrients and might not perform.

There is this feeling of – I know I need to eat a balanced diet, but I'm in a hurry.

- I need to eat now, but give me something handy and

quick so I'm on time for my classes.

- I will eat after my classes.

This is how it starts; if allowed to continue, your body suffers.

Can you set aside a day to prepare food for the upcoming week? You need to do it to stay healthy.

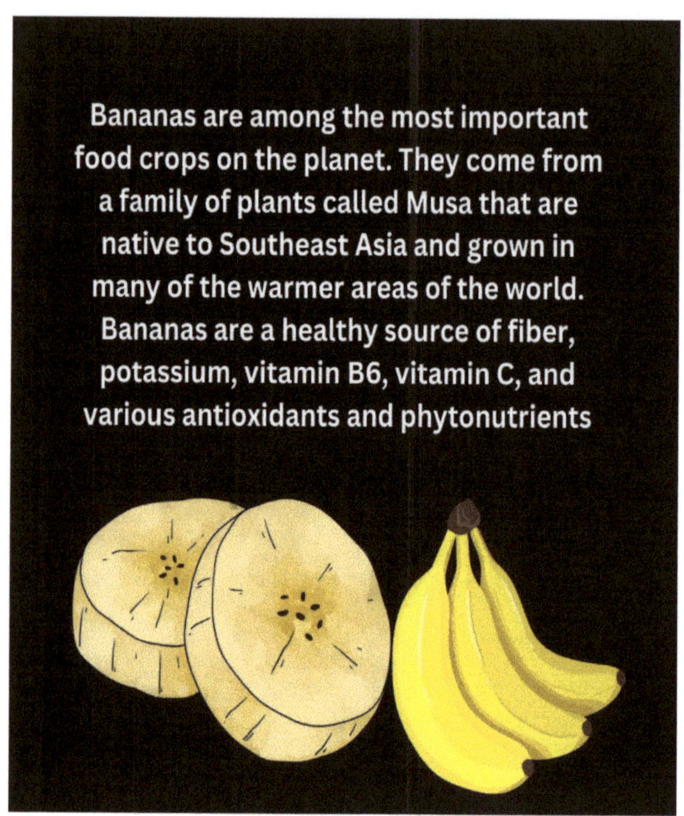

1. **Finding Food Group Balance** – try grouping certain foods and meals. There are six classes of foods and its good to know where each food ingredient belong.

   balance diet is an essential part of healthy eating.

2. **Recognizing Serving Sizes** – do you know what quantity to serve per plate or person? Knowing the right amount is vital when

dealing with whole grains, fruits, meat or fish, good fats, and milk products. This is how you can see and understand what you have consumed

3. **Learn to Read Nutrition information** – you can start reading nutrition labels to know the foods that meet your body needs.

Nutrition Facts

Serving Size oz.
Serving Per Container

Amount Per Serving:

Calories	Calories From Fat	
		% Daily value*
Total Fat		%
Saturated Fat		%
Trans Fat		
Cholesterol		%
Sodium		%
Total Carbohydrate		%
Dietary Fiber		%
Sugars		
Protein		

*Percent Daily values are based on a 2000 calorie diet. Your daily values may be higher or lewer depending on you calorie needs.

For example things like added sugar, and trans fat, check for compositions of some vitamins, essential minerals such as Vitamin C, D, Iron, magnesium and Potassium, with Fiber. This is really useful when one is sensitive to some certain foods.

How many calories should a teen eat? Teens grow very fast during puberty before they are fully grown up. Young boys develop more muscle. This usually means they require more energy (calories) to power their metabolism rate or energy usage. It's a fact that Boys typically grow faster at ages 9-14. Teen Girls will need fewer calories as they have less muscle and stop growing sooner. Moderately active teen boys need 2,200-2,800 calories daily, and girls need about 2,000, according to the guide. But it depends - calories needed change if teens are more or less active by gender and weight. For example, active boys need more calories than less active ones. The same goes for girls.

Eat whole foods, mostly plants. Avoid processed foods, but they're okay every once in a while.

Don't eat the same things all the time. Try new foods and make plates with as many colors as possible (brown beef, green broccoli, orange sweet potatoes, purple blueberries). Plan your meals whenever you can at the start of the week, and go grocery shopping only for what you need.

A well-balanced meal helps give the body the nutrition it needs to continue performing its usual tasks of development and repair.

What foods make up our healthy meals?

Carbohydrates should make up a more significant percentage of what you eat. Oats and quinoa are good sources of your carbs.

Other examples of good carbs include Whole wheat and dahlia legumes, Millet and barley, and Vegetables.

Protein:

Protein is helpful in the skin, hair, and muscle development. About 10% to 12% of your diet should consist of protein.

We have various protein sources, including legumes such as beans, soya beans, Turkey, and Poultry. Other Seafood includes fish, crab, prawns, and lobster eggs.

Lamb, beef, and pork are suitable types of lean meat.

Grecian yogurt

Avocados, nuts, and seeds are good sources of healthful fat.

Vitamins can be obtained from the following sources: fruits, vegetables, poultry, nuts, seeds, and dairy.

Minerals – your body requires minerals such as iron, calcium, potassium, iodine, and sodium, as these are necessary.

Fiber -when you take some form of fiber, it helps in food digestion while lowering your cholesterol and blood sugar levels. Further sources of fiber are lentils, quinoa, brown rice, and oats.

Water: You should drink eight glasses daily because it moisturizes your body and is necessary for several bodily processes.

You can stay away from the following foods:

"Red meat"

Maida, white bread, sewing, noodles, and pasta are examples of refined grains (cereals).

trans fat, cheese, and butter

Extra sugar

Pastry

packaged food

The most important advantage is that it satisfies the body's nutritional requirements because a balanced diet includes diverse foods.

Also, significant diseases like cancer, diabetes, and heart disease can be avoided from the beginning just by eating healthy food with the proper balance.

It helps maintain energy in the body, not only physical health. A balanced diet also helps people feel better, have more energy, and cope with stress.

Nutrients, Vitamins, Balanced Diet

Always keep the ingredients in stock. This can be fish (freezes forever) over a small bed of rice(keeps forever) with veggies(frozen bags keep forever), or a veggieburger(tends to be more nutritionally complete than normal burgers and keeps better in the freezer) with veggies(keeps forever frozen). When I say veggies, I mean actual vegetables. Tomato is a fruit, corn is a grain. Never eat corn as your vegetable.

Also, take a multivitamin. You might be missing some part of your nutrition and the amounts in those are generally enough to make up a deficiency but not enough to cause problems.

web search results:

Food Group	Examples
Carbohydrates	Fruits, vegetables, grains, bread, pasta, rice
Fats	Oils, butter, nuts, seeds, avocado, fatty meats
Protein	Lean meats, fish, eggs, dairy, beans, tofu
Fiber	Whole grains, beans, lentils, oats, bran
Dairy	Milk, yogurt, cheese, calcium-fortified alternatives
Alcohol	Wine, beer, spirits

3
Mental Health

When Mira was in junior year, she slept from two to four hours at night, skipped most of her meals and lost interest in making friends or attending classes. She felt bad and was ashamed of going for counseling. Her family members were unaware because she was an introvert. Every day, she would lay on her bed no wanting to be seen by members of her family.

Despite this, she never allowed her grades to slide.

 It got to the point that she decided to open up to her mother. At first, her mother thought it was premenstrual symptoms. This was not what she expected, further affecting her emotional state.

She had added so much weight and this made her sad. She was advised her to lose some weight by going on a regular exercise.

Using Social Media -

Popular Social media apps such as YouTube, Facebook, and Instagram are common among teens. It is estimated that 45% of teens between the ages of 13 and 17 are on social media!

There are positives and negatives to Using social media. Firstly,- Connecting with your friends, keeping in touch, and making new friends is easy. This solves some of the issues related to boredom.

- you can watch fun videos, see cute pictures, and like and share! You will find many tutorial videos online.

The Negatives

- It can be a distraction from your goals or chores.
- there are many bad things on social media. You will need to filter many of them.

- There are online Bullies who are mean and could use blackmail if they get any info about you.

- Your private information stories or images might get leaked online, and we might regret it.

Read

You can improve your fitness and keep a healthy shape by getting involve in exercises. These can be read online or through a book. After reading about these exercises, take notes and fix a time for practice.

You don't have to spend hours in the gym. There are many home workouts that are easy to do.

3. Learn new skills

When you get involved in learning a new skill, your mental health is nourished. A new skill can boost your confidence level. There are many ways to learn a skill especially from home.

Effect of exercises on the brain

According to a study done at Harvard University, exercises is seen to help the memory in two ways. Firstly, it reduces inflammation and energizes your growth hormones - these help your brain cells stay healthy and grow. You will sleep better, feel less stressed, and be in a good frame of mind.

The parts of your brain involved in thinking and remembering things get bigger when you exercise.

We have yet to determine precisely what type of exercise is best - most studies shows that aerobic exercises which increases your heart rate, e.g running, swimming, cycling, will probably have similar effects.

Do what you enjoy and stick to it. Getting active protects your brain and body from inflammation and keeps you mentally sharp - plus, working out feels awesome! What are you waiting for? Break a sweat! These things make your brain stronger!

Sleep helps the brain and body to process all that happened during the day. When you don't get enough sleep, paying attention, learning, and remembering things is harder. You also have a harder time coping when life gets stressful or emotional.

Sleep helps maintain your thinking skills to see the world clearly and handle challenges.

Get enough rest every night! Aim for 8-10 hours of good sleep. Turn off screens an hour before bed, avoid caffeine late in the day, and create a relaxing bedtime routine. Your brain and body need sleep to function at 100%. Once you develop a healthy sleep habit, you'll be energized, focused, and able to manage stress.

4

You need a Growth Mindset.

A growth mindset is a conviction that you can improve your abilities and skills using perseverance, the right methods, and the support you receive from others.

People who think they can boost their skills often succeed more than those who don't. A growth mindset means pushing yourself to learn more rather than staying in your comfort zone. Seeing possibilities instead of hurdles.

A growth mindset means you believe in your abilities to grow and become better. You have realized that your mind and skills can be developed to give you more success in all you do in life. With a bit of dedication and hard work, you can learn from your mistakes, find new ways of tackling a particular obstacle and reach more greatness.

Using a growth mindset, you can identify new opportunities and plan how to handle them with minimal risks. Now, you can move out of your comfort zone to achieve your goals faster.

A fixed mindset is the opposite of a growth mindset. In fixed mindsets, individuals think their talents are natural and set at birth. This is unlike the former, who is more concerned with self-improvement and progress through time.

People with a fixed mindset think everyone is born with certain traits, such as intellect, ability, and personality traits.

People who believe their traits are specific to their genetic makeup often also think they remain relatively the same throughout their lifetime.

This can be detrimental. Another common trait is having an aversion to taking risks. This means they may miss opportunities to learn and develop.

"CHALLENGES ALLOW ME TO GROW."

Is a Growth Mindset Adequate?

According to exciting research findings, students' motivation and academic performance can be significantly boosted by having a growth mindset.

Research studies have demonstrated how students' mindset influences various aspects of their lives, from academic achievement to engagement to willingness to challenge themselves. A successful students depends heavily on building a positive mindset!
Schools should promote a growth mindset by recognizing achievement, experimenting with various teaching methods, and seeking insightful feedback.

Reading, science, and math scores were higher for individuals with a growth mindset than those with a fixed mindset.

Growth Mindset Examples

Consider a skill you possess today that you did not have before. What prior experience did you find challenging? Why does it suddenly seem easy? And how did you do all that?

These ideas cause you to reflect on the time and effort you've put into developing specific skills, which are characteristics of a growth mindset.

Examine Other People's Achievements.

Consider anything you've seen someone else do against the odds. Consider their methods for success and what this implies about their skill development capacity.

1. Get ideas

A growth mindset may be developed by asking for input from others, regardless of whether a project succeeds. They could help you see where you need to grow or where you have made progress. This might then help you establish improvement-related objectives.

Know your weaknesses

This aspect of a fixed mindset involves accepting that

there will be abilities or disciplines in which you still need to become proficient. However, you can improve in these areas if you try and keep at it.

Knowing that your weaknesses also strengthens you still need to acquire is the first step in adopting a development mindset.

Learn any skill from scratch.

Try something new and test yourself by learning something you still need to become adept at. You may begin by studying a foreign language, playing an instrument, or mastering mathematics.

You cannot succeed if you are not willing to step out.

Make Mistakes

Allow yourself to make mistakes and learn from them. Consider mistakes as a necessary learning component rather than evidence of incompetence.

You may learn from mistakes by recognizing potential areas of weakness or ignorance where you can make

Instead of saying	Always say
i will give up trying	It's okay. I'll try again.
I'm scared of challenges.	i will learn from it
I'm not as smart as my classmate.	My classmate inspires me to study well.
it's okay	how can it be better
no need to practice	I want to improve and grow.

5

Making Friends

Let's learn from Laura, a teenager trying to make friends. Here is what she said.

I've tried joining our school's swim team, but again, everyone already has friends and inside jokes. I'm just to the side, listening. For the homework thing, I'm not really into academic stuff, which is why I ask for homework. But can you give me an example of transitioning from asking about homework to a conversation?

TIP

Practice Meeting People

I was a part of the swimming team at my school, and when I tried making new friends, everyone already had their friends. I kept taking notes since I didn't prefer to avoid discussing school topics.

Smiling and giving people a chance to talk to you is OK. However, speaking with them helps to build new relationships. You can start a conversation (a band shirt, their book, their discussion if it's appropriate to join in, anything), then continue by asking questions and demonstrating interest in who they are and what they do.

Don't pretend; be genuinely interested in others. When the chance presents itself, be approachable and get others involved in the conversation.

They'll remember you as a kind, approachable person they spoke with previously. They'll also remember you as the intriguing person who seemed at ease striking up a conversation with total strangers the next time they see you. Gee, I wish they'd come here to talk to me.

something that piques his interest. Find out if they're attending an upcoming event.

Here is how you can start up a conversation. You can ask a question. For example, "Are you coming to the party?" or "Do you like Michael Jackson songs, huh?" and then push send, followed by "I listen to them too." Perhaps include something you recently did that is relevant to the subject. People enjoy being acknowledged and getting to know others with similar interests.

Keep in mind that talks end, and discussions don't last indefinitely. If you need to do anything, take your time leaving, and let them know you'll be back shortly.

I suggest hanging out in groups. Get up to them, inquire about the source of their cool pen, and compliment it. If it goes well, you two may converse or spit. If they remain silent, keep your cool.

BE OPEN

Good friends don't necessarily know what to say, but they are good at lending an ear. There are moments when you should sit with your buddies and hear their crazy stories without giving advice.

Your friends may already know how much you care for them, but expressing it directly will make them feel more cherished. Even a brief message can have a significant effect. You may text someone, "I love you," or "I appreciate you."

Show your appreciation by complimenting them.

Friendship is a valuable gift, and you should appreciate it.

No matter what your friends are facing, be there for them. The most important thing you can do for a friend in pain is to be with them. Your presence has blessed them.

Keep in touch often.

Staying connected with friends, family, and partners requires effective communication. It's generally wise to check in with them and see how they're faring. This is relevant for both friends and couples.

Show your commitment.

Know that that if someone truly values your relationship, they will prioritize time for you, regardless of how busy they are.

Celebrate with others.

Celebrate your friends when they get a promotion, graduate with high marks, or triumph in a competition by giving them flowers or a gift.

Why not take a break with your friends to relax and forget your stresses? Build upon your memories by creating new ones.

6

Haircare tips

What is the best hair care routine for teens?

Different Hair Care Routines:

Caring for your hair as a teen is so much easier using the right products and tips for your hair type make all the difference.

Let's break down the main hair types and how to care for each:

Straight Hair

Easy to work with and popular, straight hair can get greasy since oils from your scalp can travel down easier. This also makes it fall flat and look lifeless.

- Wash every 2-3 days with a sulfate-free shampoo to limit excess grease
- Only wash hair as needed, so your scalp makes the right oil amount
- Use a coconut oil conditioner to hydrate hair and give it body
- For flat hair, use volumizing mousse to add depth and thickness
- If ponytails are drooping, spray in texturizer to hold the shape

Wavy Hair

Wavy hair can be tricky – it shares straight and curly hair issues. You may deal with a greasy scalp but dry ends. The proper routine keeps waves polished.

- Wash wavy hair every 3-4 days to balance moisture
- Dry with a soft T-shirt to prevent frizz
- Condition to nourish hair and enhance waves
- Massage in coconut oil before washing to boost volume
- Use moisturizing serums on ends
- Braid waves before bed to define them
- Scrunch in leave-in conditioner to bring out waves

Curly Hair

The right tips prevent dryness and keep curls defined. Curly hair needs specialized care.

- Use moisturizing, sulfate-free products to avoid stripping natural oils
- Only wash 2X a week to prevent dryness
- Always condition after shampooing
- Diffuse curly hair after washing to enhance curl shape
- Define curls with cream or serum
- Carefully detangle with a wide-tooth comb

Caring for your hair as a teen gets much easier when you know what you're working with!

Follow the tips for your hair type, and you'll love your looks.

Cuts Are Crucial

First rule: no DIY haircuts! I know bangs are tempting, but leave the snipping to the pros. One wrong cut could take years to fix.

Instead, get regular trims every six weeks. It won't make your hair grow faster, but it will protect existing growth. Trims help because the part you style and dye is the hair shaft. The hidden root is where growth happens. So, cuts don't change the growth rate. But they keep the shaft protected.

Over time, shaft cuticles can crack, leading to split dry ends. Trims nip damage so hair stays healthy. They also let you chat with stylists about easy 'dos, like a shag, to cut morning routines.

Hydrate Hair

Dry, curly hair is a big teen issue. When cuticles separate, hair can't hold moisture. Combine with dry scalp and too much washing, and hair dries out.

Your scalp makes natural oils to hydrate hair. But some types, like curly, tend to be drier.

Don't over-shampoo - wash frequency depends on your hair and activity. Sweat more = wash more.

Hydration Hacks

Use light oils like acai, argan, jojoba, and carrot oils with vitamins A & E to hydrate. Apply a little to dry ends and work upwards. But don't overdo oils or make your hair look greasy.

For deep conditioning, Magic Sleek Repair brings intense hydration.

Accept your hair

Embrace the hair you have, and don't be afraid to style it in a way YOU love - even if it's not "natural" for you! Use 100% formaldehyde-free treatments for curls or straightening. And go easy on hot tools to limit damage. You can completely transform your look with cuts, colors, braids - the works!

Easy Hair Care Tips

Use a conditioner

We have different types of hair conditioners. A Leave-in-conditioner adds moisture to the hair

To prevent hair damage, wring out excess water from the hair and allow to air dry.

You need a shampoo

Have you used a shampoo which keeps moisture? It helps the hair retain it natural vitamins.

What about cold water?

Wash hair with warm or cold water.

Do not use hot water as this might cause splitting, dehydrated hair or loss of hair in future.

Get a good hair cut

Your hair grows, plan on having a nice haircut. There are many styles you can choose from. just visit a barber or hair stylist to find out more.

7

Personal Hygiene

Personal hygiene is caring for our physical bodies. When you are caring for your bodies, you will wash your hands, brushing your teeth, and take your bath. Good hygiene will keep you free from germs, bacteria and you will live a healthy life.

Although our bodies do contact germs whenever we touch or play in the field or at home, we can be clean if we do simple things to stay clean so we do not become sick.

CYNTHIAS STORY

At age 10, I went through a major anti-hygiene phase and refused to brush my hair or even shower.
So, every morning and night, my mom would force me till I got out of bed. She would brush my teeth, and help me take my bath

This went on for two weeks. One day, she forgot to brush my teeth. I was sitting in class when she came bursting into the classroom waving a toothbrush. When she got closer, she said "Sweetie! We forgot to brush this morning; that's my fault!" Then, right there, she starts brushing my teeth in front of everyone!

My classmates were falling out of their seats laughing while I was pushing her away, crying. When she finally stops, she says, "If you brushed your teeth, I wouldn't have to do this!"

So yeah, I got teased for weeks and hated my mom for it. But after that incident, I started showering, brushing, flossing - anything to avoid a repeat!

the public humiliation was the wake-up call I needed. No way am I letting Mom come at me with a toothbrush again!

Bath Daily

Use a gentle soap and wash from head to toe. Remember the folds and crevices. Are you getting grimy foot odor? Thoroughly scrub between toes. Are you having issues with body odor? Some BO is standard; go gentle on the deodorant.

Oily skin and acne got you down? Washing your face twice a day can help keep pores clear. Try a medicated cleanser if you're breaking out heavily. An oily scalp needs shampooing daily, too. Discuss severe acne with your doctor.

And clean nails matter for hygiene. Use a brush and soap under and around fingernails and toenails.

Brushing

Brush twice and floss once daily! Sugary drinks and coffees rot teeth and cause bad breath. Keep that smile sparkling and your mouth feeling fresh.

Hair Care

Shaving or waxing facial and body hair is a personal choice. Do what makes you most comfortable. Protect your skin by using proper techniques to avoid irritation if removing hair.

Shaving for boys

Most teen guys will get some facial hair. You may feel nervous about shaving, and that's okay!

Shaving can be done with different tools, cutting the hair close to the skin. Be careful since razors are sharp. But if you follow these tips, you'll stay safe:

· Always use a fresh, sharp razor

· Wash your face with warm water first to soften hairs

· Apply shaving cream, gel, or foam to protect skin

· Carefully shave in the direction hair grows

· Rinse razor between strokes

· Check for missed spots and shave again

· If you cut yourself, put tissue on it and apply ointment

Now you've got this!

Shaving Tips for Girls

Shaving can be sensitive for teen girls. Having hair is a natural process of life. Try to Focus on feeling comfortable.

Many girls first shave their legs and bikini line. You can shave during a bath or shower to soften your skin. Use female shaving products or male ones work too.

Carefully move the razor against the direction of hair growth.

When shaving, you should go slowly and avoid the genital area until you have more practice.

8

Budgeting 101 for Teens

A budget helps you take control of your cash flow so you can save up for things you want.

It's a simple plan that tracks where your money comes from (your income) and where it goes (your expenses). Budgeting allows you to set financial goals and make wise spending choices.

Why Budgeting is Crucial

Budgeting gives you power over your money instead of wondering where it went. Here's how:

☞ See precisely what you spend on food, clothes, entertainment, etc.

☞ Identify areas where you overspend so you can cut back. More savings = more options!

☞ Set aside monthly money for big purchases like concerts, video games, or a car.

☞ Gain the freedom to make your own financial choices.

For a start,

- Write down all sources of income (allowance, gifts, part-time job).
- Next, track your monthly spending - every snack, movie ticket, outfit, etc. This shows where your money is going.
- Use this information to create a personalized budget that aligns with your financial goals. Adjust as needed.

Budgeting takes some effort but pays off hugely in the long run. You've got this!

What budget best depends greatly on your money personality and situation. Here are three popular ways teens track their dough:

Traditional Budgeting

Split your money into categories like food, clothes, entertainment, etc., and decide how much to spend on each. Track what you use in real life. If you hit the limit for clothes before the month ends, you'll have to cut back or take money from another category.

Pay Yourself First

First, decide how much you want to save each month. Then, figure out what you need for needs like cell phone bills. Entertainment and shopping come last. Adjust that category instead of tapping savings if you run out before paying for wants.

Zero-Based Budgeting

Every dollar you get in a month is assigned a purpose before it's spent. Nothing is left over or unplanned at the end. Consider savings and debt payments as categories, too.

Make Your Money Work for You

See if where you spend lines up with your goals and priorities. If you want a car someday, you should cut back on deliveries and streaming services now. Look at both lowering expenses and earning more through things like part-time work.

What are the prices of chicken ?

A pack of potatoes and

2 types of vegetables you can feed 2 persons with no more than $10

Visit any supermarket of choice to get the prices.

Go to any grocery store nearby and get the prices
for the following items:

2 tins of milk

3 Loaves of bread

a cup of margarine or butter

3 Tins of baked beans

a small pasta pack

If you are preparing some spaghetti for 3 persons, what are the ingredients required? Can you state how much it cost?

Find out the prices.

What's your favorite cereal milk? Can you find out how much you can get it ?

List five foods you love eating at home.

What do they cost to make, and list out all their ingredients?

If You received $25 for feeding in a week, can you write a list of the things you would purchase and how much they cost .

Avoid Budget Pitfalls

Ask yourself:

☞ Am I overspending with my credit card?

☞ Are prices rising on needs like gas and making my plan outdated?

☞ Did I budget enough wiggle room in flexible categories?

Stick to It

Use a budgeting app or write expenses in a notebook. Envelopes labeled for categories with cash inside works too! Just regularly check in and update your plan as life changes. Don't be overwhelmed. A solid budget equals financial freedom to fund your dreams!

9

Credit report 101

A credit report is a report showing how good you have been with credit. This means it's different from a credit score. You might take this to be like a school report card and rather than your school grades been written there, they write your financial activities.

When trying to get credit, lender will ask to see your credit history. This helps them determine if you should be considered for Credit. When you borrow a loan as a beginner, your credit report is used.

Borrowing and Lending

There are many needs that arise and when we cannot come up with the required amount, we look to borrow the money. Anyone you get that do not belong to you will attract an interest.

Interest is an additional amount which is a fee collected for giving you credit. this might accumulate over time.

1. Complete the tables below by calculating the amount of interest accumulated and the total owed after 5 years. Round your answers to 2 decimal places.

$1000 at 30% interest per Year

a	Principal	Interest Added	Total Owed
1	$1000	$300	$1300
2	$ ____	$900	$3900
3	$ ____	$ ____	$ ____
4	$ ____	$ ____	$ ____
5	$ ____	$ 450	$1950

find the principal interest and total amount owed

What does a credit score mean?

Your credit score can make it easier or hard to get a loan. When you have a high credit score, it means that you can be given a load at a good interest. A low or poor credit score will affect the chances of doing so. There are situations that might make the lenders quote a higher interest rate when a poor credit score is discovered.

Credit Rating: is a rating which is assigned by lenders and used to show the type of credit you have taken. For example, a car loan has its credit rating and if you pay on time or defaulted, there is a rating assigned. **This** might be numbers or alphabets used by banks or financial institutions.

When mike approached a bank, he thought he could get a loan easily. The first thing he was asked to do was fill a form to determine his credit score and rating. Will he get the loan he applied for a will he be denied? His credit score shows that has not been paying his bills promptly.

A credit score shows if you have a good reputation of keep and managing money and if you can pay back what you borrowed. For example, If you borrow $20 from me and pay it back on time, you will earn more of my as I can lend you more money later.

Three big companies keep track of everyone's repayment history and give scores from 0 to 900 to show how reliable they think you are. Over 700 means you're decent at paying back debts. 900 is as good as it gets.

To build good credit, you have to handle loans responsibly - make payments on time, never miss a month. Doing this raises your score. Messing up payments tanks your score. People work on "building credit" so that later on, banks will approve bigger loans with lower interest rates.

Here's a real life example: Stan and Kyle each owed $1000 on credit cards for game systems. Kyle paid back everything, with interest, in two months. But it took Stan five years because he spent money on other stuff instead. Now both guys want a $20,000 car and need to borrow more. The bank approves a loan for Kyle at 8% interest since his repayment history shows reliability. Stan has to pay 14% interest because of his spotty credit history. He can take the loan or not.

It's better to borrow only what you can pay back. Start small with a phone plan, then a credit card, then big loans for cars or a house. That's how you build strong credit.

Defaulting in any money you have borrowed will affect your credit score. this is the reason why we strive to gain higher credit rating and score.

As you grow, learn basic rules about money. lenders check your credit score to decide whether to trust you and what interest rate to give. Good credit means better rates.

It's confusing at first. Say I never missed a payment on my cards and loans. My high score makes lenders think, "Jessica pays bills on time. Let's approve her loan application." But what if I can't actually afford a new loan payment?

If I were lending money, I'd want proof of income and current debts, not just a score. A credit score doesn't show your full money situation. But it gives lenders a quick snapshot of how you handled loans so far.

To calculate your score, agencies use percentages:

- 35% based on payment history - do you pay bills on time?

- 30% based on credit usage - what percent of your limit is used?

- 15% on length of credit history - how long have you had loans?

The key for a teen is just to start some credit by paying a phone bill. Then get a card and always pay on time. Good credit takes time but pays off!

10

Cooking Skills

Do You Enjoy Watching your parents make delicious meals? I know we have all been there since the best meals we might have seen are those of our parents. As you grow, learn how to succeed and make good cooking decisions in the kitchen. We have outlined eight cooking techniques teenagers should know:

Boiling

Making pasta, rice, boiling potatoes, and cooking vegetables requires boiling water in a pan without drying it out or bubbling over. Although learning is simple, it's the first step in every culinary adventure.

EGGS

Eggs can be fried or cooked. When you know how to make eggs may save your breakfast. You'll always have something to eat when there is scrambled eggs, fried eggs, poached eggs, omelets, and the rest in your locker! And you'll always have the means to pay for a balanced lunch.

CHOPPING fruits and vegetables

Develop effective vegetable cutting techniques since doing it incorrectly may be taxing and deadly. Knowing where and how to position your fingertips is essential because sloppy finger placement may hurt you and damage ingredients for everyone else.

Safely handling fruits:

When good fruits are eating, it repairs our body immune system and this is a vital part of out health. This keeps you from falling sick since Here's what you need to know:

Start cutting

- select fresh, ripe fruit free from bruises, mold, or insect damage. skip fruit which might seem to have rot.

- do not keep them close to raw meat or chemicals in your cart and bags. Protect your meat by wrapping them so fruit juices don't touch fruit.

Storing

- Don't wash fruit before storing it. Wash right before you eat it.

- Keep stored fruit in a cool, dry, dark place, not near heat or sunlight. Don't put heavy stuff on top of it.

- Once cut, you can transfer them to the refrigerator. Place them in seal bags or containers.

Preparing

- Wash your hands and clean the surfaces before you begin or when you are through handling fruit.

- Scrub when the fruit has a hard coat but rub gently when it's a soft coated fruit. You shouldn't use soap. Remove outer leaves of lettuce/cabbage.

- A good cutting board and knives will be handy in this work

- keep in the fried for within 2 hours of cutting.

Following these basic safety tips will help you enjoy delicious healthy fruit without worrying about getting sick. Be smart when handling fruit!

Roasting

when it comes to cooking meat properly, you should know the difference between beef/lamb and chicken/pork. Beef and lamb can be served rare or pink in the middle and still be safe to eat. But chicken and pork need to cook all the way through until there's no pinker showing. An easy way to remember this: If your chicken or pork still looks pink inside, pop it back in the oven for a bit longer. You don't want to risk getting sick from undercooked poultry or pig.

Cooking the right way takes some skill but it's so worth learning. Not only will your food taste better, but you'll be safer from illness too. Plus, your friends and family will be super impressed with your mad kitchen abilities! Being able to whip up tasty meals on a budget is essential these days with high food costs and all those tempting takeaways on every corner.

So take some time to build your cooking skills - it's a gift to yourself and others that pays off over and over.

A good cooking skill is an important thing for teens to learn. Plan out meals for the whole week that work with your budget. Do you know how to make a detailed shopping list to get just what you need without overspending? Being organized about ingredients and recipes before you shop is key.

There's more to it than just shopping. Have you learned the fundamentals of working in the kitchen like preparing ingredients, proper storage methods, reheating food safely, and cleaning up?

Building these knife skills will give you confidence to cook a wider variety of foods instead of relying on someone else to cook for you or only eating packaged and takeout food all the time. Conquering the fear of knives in the kitchen opens up so many recipe possibilities!

Here are some other essential cooking skills every teen should work to master:

Making Eggs – Learning different methods like scrambling, frying, poaching, boiling and making omelets means endless quick, tasty and affordable meal options with eggs as the protein-packed base. Experiment with add-ins like veggies, cheese, meat crumbles or salsa to build even more flavor.

Salads – Salads can move beyond sad, boring side dish status with the right mix of textures and flavors. Start with sturdy leafy greens then pile on the veggies, add a carbohydrate element like beans or pasta, mix in protein from sliced grilled chicken or hardboiled eggs, drizzle on a flavorful dressing and finish with crunchy toppers like homemade croutons, seeds or shaved parmesan cheese. With planning, salads make amazing one-dish meals.

Leftovers – Getting comfortable working with leftovers saves tons of money and reduces food waste. Think outside the box on ways to transform last night's leftovers into new tasty meals. Casseroles, stir fries, frittatas, sandwiches, soups and salads are all smart ways to give leftovers new life. Taking leftovers for lunch means quicker prep compared to making something new.

Spices/Herbs/Sauces –

Having flavor boosters on hand like lemon juice, soy sauce, fresh garlic, Italian seasoning and Sriracha means you can add excitement to even the simplest veggie side dish or boring piece of leftover chicken. Build up your home spice collection to easily enhance dishes without needing a recipe.

Freezing/Thawing/Reheating –

Learn best practices for food safety when working with the freezer. Know what foods freeze well and the proper techniques to freeze, thaw and then reheat items without ruining texture and taste. Frozen foods prepared at home are way healthier than processed frozen meals and snacks from the grocery store too.

Plant-based meals –

Incorporate more vegetables and vegan recipes into your cooking repertoire. Going meatless more often saves money and helps increase your fruit and vegetable intake. Having some vegetarian meal ideas at the ready means you always have options when cooking for yourself or others who don't eat meat.

Mastering these kitchen fundamentals now will serve you well as you eventually transition into cooking more completely for yourself. Self-sufficiency feels great! Don't let cooking intimidate you. Start simple, get hands-on practice with essential techniques and build up your confidence over time.

Baking reduces tension and is another way to use leftover fruit, vegetables, and bread. For example, our Bread and Butter Pudding Muffins are a delicious way to use leftover bread and are rich in dried fruits and toasty spices.

We all make mistakes in the kitchen sometimes. We burn ourselves (or our food), cut our fingers with a sharp knife, and occasionally, meals don't come out how we want. It's how we learn; sometimes, the tastiest meals are total food accidents.

Have the courage to inquire; excellent chefs always get advice and recipes from friends, family, and recognized authorities. Even after years of cooking for my family and eighteen years of operating a culinary school, I still study recipe books, attend demonstrations, and inquire if I need clarification. I learned how to cook by watching my mom prepare food as a small child (and later by assisting her).

Last but not least, have fun! You will spend much time on food-related activities, including cooking for yourself, for four and a half years. Identify the dishes that make you happy and learn how to prepare them effectively.

11

Mindfulness for Teens:

Being mindful is paying close attention to your thoughts, your emotions, and all physical perceptions on purpose taking the present moment with curiosity.
For example, If You Are in a room. and you could hear sounds from nearby building, you could also hear your neighbor next door crying. these things are all happening at the same time.

This is mindfulness

You can separate what events you well on about life and the priority we place on them. You know that whatever you're worrying about isn't that important anyway by taking a step back (mindfulness) and placing that your true nature is an empty, accepting space.

USING YOUR MINDFUL SENSES

INSTRUCTIONS 

I SEE..

Look around and notice the colors, shapes, and patterns in your surroundings.
Write down at least three things you see, and briefly describe what catches your eye.

I HEAR..

Listen carefully to the sounds around you. What can you hear? Write down at least three distinct sounds, and note how they make you feel. 

I SMELL..

Identify any scents in the air. What can you smell? Describe at least three different smells and their characteristics. 

I FEEL..

Explore the sense of touch by reaching out and feeling various objects or surfaces.
Describe the textures and sensations you experience when touching things like leaves, rocks, or tree bark. 

Why mindfulness is a good thing to practice:

You can be free from worrying of past situations. Do not allow these things get to you. Some of these worries might appear unimportant but linger in your mind for years when you are not watching. Mindfulness involves acknowledging that you can't change some situations. This is what helps you live in the present, as mentioned in the paragraph above. The present because you aren't concerned about the past or the future.

Practicing mindfulness might not be easy. You will always find challenges which might want to frustrate you. If you don't deal with these feelings, you'll keep imagining scenarios to avoid them. This will only worsen the problem.

It's normal to struggle at first with mindfulness.

When I started practicing mindfulness, I Experienced significant changes in health. I simply did what I learned and started decluttering my mind from negative and unhealthy thoughts. This means that I would move outside my comfort zone and try new things. When I began schooling, I was too busy to be mindful and did not really have much time to do much meditation. My mental health suffered, and I began having unhealthy thought patterns again.

So mindfulness is effective, but as I mentioned, maintaining it and reaping its benefits requires effort.

Mindfulness can be practiced at any time of the day as a way of life.

Practice being mindful as you are eating. Choose how you prepare and arrange your food or how it was grown, and who might have helped with its production, harvesting, or preparation.

<u>What's are you thinking about today?</u>

Emotion regulation is better. You can get involve in doing physical, mental, emotional, or spiritual mindfulness.

Take a deep breath.

Breathing is a traditional mindfulness practice that involves controlling the breath while paying conscious attention to it. The breathing discussed here is slow, deep breathing that activates the diaphragm. Your body relaxes.

1. Paced breathing (for example, inhale five, exhale seven)

Paced breathing, in which the duration of inhaling and exhaling is deliberately altered, is another breathing method. Because our pulse rate decreases during exhalation, it might be beneficial to have a longer exhalation than an inhalation. Try breathing in for five counts and out for seven. Make sure your breaths are diaphragmatic by using the techniques from the earlier exercises (deep breathing).

THE WAY I FEEL NOW...

Color the jars according to how you feel today.

1.

Relax your muscles.

Tensing and relaxing specific muscle groups is called progressive muscle relaxation. Put as much strain on your neck and shoulders, for instance, by scrunching them up to your ears. Count slowly to three to let out all that stress. Do the same with your hands, arms, chest, stomach, and other muscles. Depending on your preferences, you may exercise larger or smaller muscle groups.

1. Meditation

There are several meditation habits, all of which require maintaining a single physical posture and focusing on a single aspect. This could be your breathing, a mantra, or bodily sensations. Bring your attention back to that focus whenever your mind wanders—and it will—without passing judgment. Meditating may not be suitable for all ages and might be painful at first. It's OK to try alternative mindfulness exercises if this one makes you uncomfortable.

1. Using 5-4-3-2-1 as grounding.

Teens, or anyone of any age, are brought back to the present moment via all of their senses by the 5-4-3-2-1 exercise.

Observe and declare aloud or silently:

Choose five objects of that color, like five blue things.

Four sensations you might experience

(such as the chair's back against yours or the chilly air
on your hands)

Three noises are audible.

Two items that you can smell (Actively smelling things is OK, such as washing detergent on your clothing.)

one flavor you love.

Body Scan

Body scans are another easy mindfulness exercise. Spend 10 to 30 seconds focusing on each area of your body, such as your toes, the soles of your feet, or the tops of your feet. All bodily sensations, including warmth, cold, pressure, tension, tingling, pain, or texture, should be noted. There are several guided body scans available to make this easier.

journaling

Especially when uncensored, journaling is thoughtful. When journaling, you may "free write," which means write whatever comes to mind without editing or censoring. Using prompts might help direct your writing toward certain subjects.

1. Activity/Exercise

When done with complete concentration, repeated exercises may become meditative. When performed with a mindfulness-based mindset, almost any physical activity may be transformed into a mindfulness exercise. Take a stroll while paying attention to everything around you, such as noises, temperature, walking sensations, and the local nature.

1. Using color

Coloring is a simple mindfulness exercise. Coloring may add creativity and fun to mindfulness. Concentrate entirely on the colors to make this exercise meaningful. Softly and without criticism, bring the focus back to coloring whenever the mind wanders.

1. Take a music break.

Give your favorite music your undivided attention. You may listen to everything blindfolded. Try to pay attention to how music affects your emotions.

1. Eat mindfully

Try carefully eating fruit or candy for a quick mindfulness exercise. Start with a clementine; observe the fruit's color, texture, and scent, then gently peel it. Examine the sensation of picking it up after eating.

Teenagers may maintain mindfulness habits in eight ways:

Find something you like doing since practicing will be much easier. It's OK if one mindfulness exercise doesn't seem right. Find something you enjoy and try another.

Maintain a moderate pace. If mindfulness practice is too demanding, shorten it. If it's just 1, 2, or 5 minutes, that's OK too! Twenty minutes of meditation and 5 minutes of coloring each day are beneficial. Allow mindfulness to develop naturally by starting small.

Pair it with an existing habit: Habit experts say matching your behavior with an existing one might help it stick. For instance, brush your teeth mindfully every morning. Or, if you usually read before bed, do some deep breathing just before. 8

Create a reward for the habit. By coming up with a reward, you may help the habit stick. 8 You need a motivational incentive, so consider using a habit-tracking app where you can mark your accomplishments. You could reward yourself with a Starbucks beverage each time you finish your mindfulness practice.

Choose the proper time of day since not everyone thrives in the morning or at night. This is terrific. Use this information to finish your mindfulness practice when it is most conducive to your energy. For instance, only do it in the morning if you're well rested.

Consider varying it if you find it challenging to maintain the same daily routine. Create a list of mindfulness exercises. You may make it as short or long as you desire, but experiment.

Create an alarm or reminder using your phone or a smart speaker, and set it at the best time for you.

12

Body Image

A negative body image is having a bad image of yourself. Anyone who has a bad image about themselves portray a low self-esteem.

Positive body image is associated with high self-esteem, comfort, and self-confidence.

The National Eating Disorders Association has listed ten steps to a positive body image:

Be grateful for all you have. You are one step closer to your goals every day. Celebrate the beautiful things your body does for you, such as letting you run, dance, breathe, laugh, and dream.

Create a list of the top 10 qualities you value most about yourself,

____

____

____

____

____

____

____

unrelated to your weight or appearance. Read your list often. As you discover additional positive characteristics about yourself, add them.

BODY-POSITIVE WORDS

1. Every day, I remind myself that I am worthy of love.

2. I refuse to let societal judgments limit my potential or dampen my spirit.

3. My worth is not defined by the appearance of my physical form.

4. I am embracing every curve, line, and imperfection as a testament to my unique beauty and worth.

Show your body that you respect it by doing something kind for yourself. Find a quiet area outdoors to unwind, take a bubble bath, and schedule sleep.

Help others with the time and energy you would have spent worrying about food, calories, or weight. Reaching out to others can boost your self-esteem and positively impact the world.

What factors affect body image?

Research shows that various things influence a child's or an adolescent's body image. These factors impact your body image:

Psychological characteristics:

Research shows that body image dissatisfaction is not isolated. Therefore, worry, melancholy, and a sense of being out of control are more frequent among kids and teenagers with poor body image.

Family: Girls with overweight parents have lower self-esteem and feel less physically capable. Furthermore, teens take after their parents' body image. Considering this, the research focused on children whose mothers discussed body image issues. The researchers also discovered that these kids perceive their bodies poorly.

Peers: Teens' peers' mindsets and viewpoints impact their body image. That includes peers of all ages. In one study, fifth- and sixth-graders who attended schools with older students had more negative body images. This was contrasted with females of the same age attending a school with younger pupils.

Celebrity: It is known that the media harms young people's body image. According to the "Ideal to Real" body image poll, 80% of young females relate their appearances to celebrities. Additionally, almost half of those females said seeing celebrities makes them self-conscious about their appearance.

Teens who use social media often contrast their bodies with staged photos of their friends and famous people. Social media has been connected to melancholy, narcissism, and adolescent body-image disorders because of the accompanying sense of failure.

Daily

AFFIRMATIONS

I am confident and comfortable in my own skin

I'm so grateful for all of the adventures I experience daily

I have released my attachment to the desires of the ego

I am the best version of myself

I welcome opportunities to learn and grow

A Common Sense Media poll found that 35% of kids who use social media worry about being identified in unappealing pictures. Furthermore, 27% of people worry about their appearance when publishing images. And 22% say they feel self-conscious when no one "likes" or comments on their pictures. Boys also report experiencing the same emotions; females report having them more often.

In 13-year-old research titled "Being Thirteen," individuals who viewed social networking websites 50 to 100 times daily were 37% more upset than those who checked less often. Facebook usage has also been associated with increased eating problems. It brings together some risk-increasing elements: poor self-esteem, media images, and peer pressure.

This also holds for young adults and older teenagers. In a study released in 2016, researchers in the United States spoke with 881 female college students. Therefore, they discovered youths compared their bodies more to those of their peers the more time they spent on social media. As a result, individuals had negative body image feelings. In addition, a 2017 study found that sharing and taking selfies lowers self-worth.

Self-Esteem and Body Image

Your body image improves when you accept your body as it is. Also, your sense of worth

But what if I need to improve my fitness level? Some people believe they can enjoy their physique when they are in better shape. But it's better to go the other way. Accept your body first. Discover its positives. Maintain your health. It is easier to care for your body if you enjoy it.

Do you want to feel and look your best? Here is some advice:

13

Laundry and Clothes

Being a teen comes with lots of challenges. There are so many chores and activities to do all within the same day or week. Washing your clothes is one of such thing. Many parents are also careful so that their washer is not destroyed in the process. So how do you get this dirt of your clothes and stay clean.

Simple Steps to Laundry

- Separate the clothes into dark colors, whites, permanent press clothes, delicates, and jeans, etc.
- Always check the labels of some of the clothes to see if you will find specific directions.

for any specific washing directions; if there are none, use cold water to clean the item.

- Open some of the cloth pocket to see if you left anything in it, also recheck them before placing them into the washing machine.

As you wash ensure that the spin cycle is adequately aligned to the washer.

So after adjusting the water temperature and level, start the machine.

- Pour in your detergent and also you may add softeners.
- When it's done washing, you can follow best drying directions.
- Hang the clothes to dry or use a dryer.
- Make your temperature control selections, then start the machine after checking and emptying the lint collector.

STEPS TO WASH WELL

1. Prepare the laundry detergent and pour into water

2. wash the clothes that are stained with dirt

3. rinse carefully in clean plain water

4. Dry clothes

Common laundry mistakes

Sometimes, when washing, we might forget removing valuable things from the pockets.

When to start?

Other benefits of Laundry

It develops executive function abilities, such as initiating and completing a project, managing time, planning, setting priorities, and having foresight. These are just a few. Besides valuable tools, the Occupational Therapist's Toolbox offers an in-depth training course on executive function.

The activity may be changed to accommodate the participant's level, considering factors such as motor planning, executive functioning skills, physical capabilities, etc.

It helps one become more self-reliant and independent.

HOW TO DEVELOP LAUNDRY LIFE SKILLS

Create a laundry checklist – things you will need

1. Separate light clothing & dark clothing into two different piles

2. Put 1 pile into washing machine.

3. Do not fill washing machine more than 3/4 of the way full

4. Measure detergent & put it into __________

5. Close lid

6. Turn washing machine on

7. Push ________________ button

8. Press start

9. Put into dryer when it is done

Before Laundry, gently scrape the deodorant off a washcloth.

Wash everything cold, and let items dry naturally. I know it sounds funny, but I hang-dry my underwear. After all, I want them to last because I spend some money on each pair, purchasing from ethical businesses. I use the dryer for household stuff, socks, and sleep shirts.

 My nice clothing doesn't go in the dryer. Still, occasionally, I notice that some items that hang dry become wrinkled and stiff, like t-shirts. If that happens, I'll throw it in the dryer for 10 minutes to soften it back up (or hang it somewhere outside where it moves as it dries).

Baking soda, Dawn dish soap, and hydrogen peroxide can be applied, gently scrubbed in, and left to soak for 30 minutes to treat stains and odors before being placed in the usual Laundry. I used this on white shirts after each wear to prevent armpit odors and stains. If you still need to wash and dry it, this method works wonders on any stain.

If you need to wash a stain off your shirt, jeans, or another item under water, place the unstained side up and the stained side down. The force of the water drives the stain from the fabric. It may sound strange, but it is effective. I had only recently used it to wash a blowout from my baby's clothes.

Always carefully check your machine's settings before pushing the start button, especially if you recently finished a load of sheets and towels. It's a simple habit, but it's stupid. I've unintentionally loaded the hot cycle with Laundry since I had just finished running the towels in the load before.

References

1.) Golbidi, S., Daiber, A., Korac, B., Li, H., Essop, M. F., & Laher, I. (2017). Health benefits of fasting and caloric restriction. **Current diabetes reports, 17**(12), 123.

2.) Dinu, M., Abbate, R., Gensini, G. F., Casini, A., & Sofi, F. (2017). Vegetarian, vegan diets and multiple health outcomes: a systematic review with meta-analysis of observational studies. **Critical reviews in food science and nutrition, 57**(17), 3640-3649.

3. The Neuroscience of Growth Mindset and Intrinsic Motivation - PMC (nih.gov) research work

9 781100 219356